The Secret Mermaid

Seaside Adventure

Sue Mongredien

USBORNE

The Secret Mermaid

Seaside Adventure

Sue Mongredien

Illustrated by Maria Pearson

USBORNE

For Tom Powell, who helped
with lots of animal facts in this story.

First published in the UK in 2009 by Usborne Publishing Ltd., Usborne House,
83-85 Saffron Hill, London EC1N 8RT, England. www.usborne.com

A CIP catalogue record for this book is available from the British Library.

FMAMJJASOND/19

ISBN 9780746096161   02961-3

Printed in India

Contents

The Mermaids of the

Molly

Ella

Delphi

Shivana

Undersea Kingdom

Coral

Queen Luna

Princess Silva

Pearl

Chapter One

Molly Holmes fastened the last button on her pyjama top and sat down on her bed with a loud yawn.

"Sounds like someone's ready for a good night's sleep," Molly's dad said, ruffling her hair. "All that sea air's worn you out, Molls!"

Molly smiled up at her dad, whose head almost touched the sloping white ceiling of her attic bedroom. He was right – she'd been on the beach all day again, paddling, swimming, and building huge castles and moats in the sand. Horseshoe Bay was certainly a magical place to be...in more ways than one!

"It still feels like we're on holiday," she confessed. "I keep forgetting that we actually live here now."

Her mum and gran came into the room just then, and both smiled at Molly's words.

"I know what you mean," her dad replied, glancing around the room. "It's strange for me too, being back. I've always thought of this room as my old bedroom, from when I was a boy. Now it's yours." He grinned at her.

"I think that's a good thing, though, don't you?"

Molly nodded. It had only been a few days since she and her family had come to live with Gran in her seaside cottage, The Boathouse. Molly hadn't wanted to leave her old home and school friends at first, but she was surprised how quickly she was settling into Horseshoe Bay. What was more, she'd already made some very special secret friends...the mermaids of the Undersea Kingdom!

Molly's mum crossed the room to close the curtains. "Look how high the tide is," she remarked in surprise, gazing out. "Does it usually come up that far?"

Gran went over to the window. She walked slowly and had to lean on a stick, because she'd had a bad fall not long ago. Molly came to look out too, and stood between her mother and grandmother to stare down at the sea.

Molly's new bedroom definitely had the best view! She could see the whole of Horseshoe Bay from her window, and loved gazing out at the small cove, with its black rocks, soft golden sand, and sailing boats going by. Tonight, the waves had surged right up to the rocks, lapping at the shiny dark boulders with white foamy tongues.

Gran's forehead was crinkled in a little frown. "It does seem very high," she agreed. "Beth next door told me there's been flooding further along the coast, too. It's very unusual for this time of year."

"Flooding?" Molly echoed anxiously.

"Yes," said Gran. She looked worried for a moment as she watched the waves, then put a hand on Molly's shoulder. "We'll be all right here," she said reassuringly. "We're too high up to be flooded. I promise we won't get washed away any time soon!"

"Your gran's right," Molly's dad said. "This house has been here for hundreds of years. It's seen off a few high tides before."

"Anyway," Molly's mum said, pulling the curtains closed, "it's time you were in bed, Molly Holmes, and fast asleep. In you hop!"

Molly went back to her bed and folded her

legs under the covers. Her mum, dad and gran all came over and kissed her goodnight, before turning to leave the room. Gran blew a last kiss from the doorway and then gently shut the door.

Once she was alone, Molly stretched out a hand to the bedside table nearby and groped around in the darkness, her heart thumping as her fingers found a smooth, cool object. There it was! The piece of conch shell on a

silver chain that Gran had given her the day they had arrived. But not just any old piece of shell. A magical shell that had taken her on a wonderful mermaid adventure that very first night!

Molly could still hardly believe what had happened – it had been so amazing! To think that she had actually become a mermaid with her very own sparkling tail, *and* had met Queen Luna and the other mermaids, in the Merqueen's palace under the sea. There Molly had heard the full story about her special shell. And – most exciting of all – she'd discovered that she was a "secret mermaid", descended from a line of girls going back through the years that included Molly's gran – and now Molly!

But two nights had passed since then and nothing more had happened. Was she doing something wrong? Had she missed some crucial instruction from the Merqueen about how to get back to the Undersea Kingdom? She couldn't even ask Gran about it, as she was sworn to secrecy about her adventure. Was she *ever* going to be a mermaid again?

Molly stared up at the ceiling, listening to the crashing waves outside, and remembered Gran's worried face as she'd looked out of the window. She hoped her new friends were all right. She knew that they, and the rest of their ocean world, were in danger from Carlotta, a bad mermaid known as the Dark Queen. What if this flooding was something to do with her?

She sighed, winding the silver chain neatly around the conch and setting it on her pillow. "Please let me see the mermaids again," she whispered to it. "Please!" Then she wriggled into a more comfortable position and lay still for a few moments. She was just closing her eyes to go to sleep when she thought she heard her name being called very faintly by a faraway voice. *Molly... Molly... Molly...*

She opened her eyes at once...and gasped in excitement. The air around the conch was glittering with hundreds of tiny golden sparkles, and a warm pink light shone out from the curved shell. The mermaid magic must be starting again!

Chapter Two

Just as quickly as it had appeared, the pink
light vanished, and Molly lay in the darkness.
Now what? She was still here, a girl in her
bed. Hadn't the magic worked?

Her heart pounded as she tried to think.
She knew the mermaids could only call to her
while she slept. So maybe if she closed her
eyes again...

Crossing her fingers hopefully, Molly shut

her eyes – and immediately felt as if she were falling through the air at great speed.

Something's happening! she thought in delight, not daring to open her eyes. She could hear a bubbling sound in her ears, then felt as if her body was dissolving somehow. Then she could feel the cool water against her skin and knew she was back in the Undersea Kingdom once more.

She opened her eyes and looked down to where her legs usually were. They had vanished, and in their place flicked a beautiful, long mermaid tail, its scales sparkling a bright emerald green. On her top half, Molly was wearing a turquoise top, and her shell necklace was around her throat. Yes! She was a mermaid again! She turned a watery somersault, laughing in joy as the world spun before her. Then she paused and looked around. Where *was* she anyway?

It only took Molly a moment to recognize the pretty underwater courtyard garden that was part of the Merqueen's palace. There was the pink scallop shell where Queen Luna had sat to explain to Molly that, as the secret mermaid, she was one of six special mermaids called Shell-Keepers. Each Shell-Keeper looked after a magical piece of conch shell – until Carlotta, the Dark Queen, had stolen every piece except Molly's, that was. But then somehow, magically, the five captured shell pieces had escaped from the Dark Queen's cave, and were now lost and scattered throughout the ocean. Molly had to help the other Shell-Keepers find them before Carlotta got to them first.

Just then, Molly heard a familiar voice nearby. "I've called you here because— Ahh, Molly! Welcome!"

The voice belonged to Queen Luna herself.

She swam towards Molly, looking stately and
beautiful, with her golden crown perched on her
long chestnut hair, and a diamond glittering on
a golden chain around her neck.

She was followed by Ella, the very first
mermaid Molly had met, and
they both came over to
Molly and hugged her.

"I'm glad you're here," the Merqueen said. "As I was about to explain to Ella, I've just had word from some seals who think they've seen magical-looking sparkles in a coastal cave north of here. It may be nothing, of course, but we should look into it, in case it is one of the missing conch pieces. Ella, as protector of the coastline, you must investigate. Molly, you go too – but look after your conch carefully. Don't let any of the Dark Queen's servants near it!"

"Of course," Molly replied, feeling her skin prickle at the thought.

"Coral, Delphi, Pearl and Shivana are still searching for their shells in different areas of the ocean," the queen went on. "But the Dark Queen and her army are sure to be hunting for them too. There is no time to lose!"

Ella bobbed a curtsy to the Merqueen.

"We'll report back if we find
anything," she promised.
Then she grabbed
Molly's hand.
"Come on," she
said. "Let's go!"

The two friends
swam out of the
garden. Molly
loved the way she
could surge through
the water so swiftly
with the smallest of
flicks from her powerful
tail fin. Her hair streamed out
behind her, and she realized that her heart
was thumping with excitement. She was off
on another adventure in the Undersea
Kingdom. Oh, it was good to be back!

Just as they were leaving the Merqueen's courtyard, Molly caught sight of a shadowy figure at the edge of the garden and recognized the dark hair and shimmering purple cape of Princess Silva, the queen's daughter. Molly was surprised to see her. How long had the princess been there in the shadows? she wondered.

But before she could think any more about it, they were surging through the gleaming front doors of the palace, and Ella was speaking to her.

"My piece of the conch helps look after the coastline and tides, along with the magic of the moon," she was saying. "I really hope that it's my piece of shell in the coastal cave! Ever since the Dark Queen stole it from me, the tides have been out of control. They're either too high, causing floods, or too low, leaving sea plants and creatures in danger of drying out."

Molly remembered what her parents and gran had been saying earlier. "There have been floods near us, our neighbour said," she told Ella as they swerved to avoid a shoal of tiny electric-blue fish. "And just as I was going to bed, my mum noticed the tide was really high."

Ella looked unhappy at Molly's words. "It's even more important that we find my shell, then," she replied. "Once it's back with me, the tides will turn smoothly, and all will be well. But if the shell stays lost, or falls into the hands of Carlotta again..."

She didn't finish her sentence, but she didn't need to; her mournful shrug said it all. Then she squared her shoulders and Molly saw a flash of determination in her eyes. "Still," she went on, "you never know, maybe the seals really *have* found my shell. And then I'll be able to calm the tides straight away."

Ella swam faster at the thought, and Molly had to push her strong tail extra-hard to keep up. They swam at great speed through the gates that marked the boundary of the Undersea Kingdom, and travelled further out to sea, passing a pod of frolicking dolphins, colourful coral reefs that heaved with bright fishes, and great forests of red and brown seaweed that swayed beneath them.

"Nearly there," Ella said, and then pointed ahead. "Ahh – look, there they are."

Molly peered through the water and saw a group of sleek seals, with wide eyes and long snouts, and mottled, silvery-grey bodies. She and Ella approached them, and Ella spoke to them in a language Molly didn't understand.

The seals listened attentively, and then the largest seal replied to her in a curious barking speech, pointing with one of his flippers.

Ella nodded gratefully when he finished, and smiled. "Thank you," she said, before waving goodbye.

"Which way do we go?" Molly asked when the seals had swum away. She was expecting Ella to lead her in the direction the seal had pointed, but to her surprise, Ella took her hand and pulled her straight up to the surface of the ocean.

Molly gasped as her head broke the water. "It's so dark!" she cried, blinking as her eyes adjusted. Below the surface, the water had been a bright azure blue, as if the sun was streaming through it, but up here, in the cool night air, the sea around them looked black, apart from ripples of silvery light reflected from the moon.

Ella's flowing blonde hair looked black too, plastered against her head. "Didn't you know?" she said. "We mermaids can see through the dark seas when we're underwater. It's only when our eyes are above the surface that we see like humans."

Molly shivered, and wiped her wet hair away from her face. "I prefer it under the water, I think," she said. "It's so cold up here."

Ella nodded. "Spoken like a true mermaid," she told Molly, with a grin. Then she pointed in front of them. "That's where we're going," she said. "The cave over there, near the beach."

The tide was high up the beach, but there was still a wide slice of sand at the top which looked silvery-grey by the light of the moon. Molly could just make out a dark hollow in the cliff face at the water's edge, which she guessed was the cave.

"Let's go," Ella said. "The quicker the better. If the shell *is* in there, we need to get to it before the Dark Queen. Come on!"

Molly plunged below the surface after Ella. Ahh! That was better! She blinked as her eyes adjusted to the light, then followed her friend as she struck out in the direction of the cave.

It was exciting, thinking that they might be close to finding Ella's shell, but Molly was also a little scared. What if the Dark Queen and her followers had heard about the strange sparkles in the cave, too? Would they be swimming this way as well?

Molly glanced around nervously. She'd already met one of the creatures loyal to the Dark Queen – a huge black octopus that had tried to snatch Molly's conch piece from around her neck with its long snaky tentacles. It had been so frightening! Luckily, the power of her shell had sent the octopus away and she'd been able to escape. She really didn't want to meet any more of the Dark Queen's army though.

"Not much further now," Ella said just then, interrupting Molly's thoughts. "We just need to... Oh!"

She broke off as there came a great rushing of water.

"What's happening?" Molly shouted in alarm – but then she saw for herself. An enormous creature was powering through the water, its eyes glowing a strange red. And it was heading straight for them!

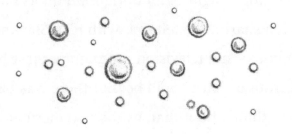

Chapter Three

Molly screamed in fright but Ella seemed too shocked to even move. "Quick!" Molly shouted, grabbing Ella's hand and pulling her out of the way.

The creature swam past, just missing them, and Molly caught sight of an upright fin on its back. Was it a shark? She felt sick with fear. She knew from books and television programmes just how dangerous a shark could be. But there was barely time to think about that, as the two mermaids were both swept along in the powerful wake that followed the huge creature. Molly's heart was pounding as she stared after it.

No, it wasn't a shark. It was mostly jet-black, but with a brilliant white belly, and white patches on the sides of its head. "What *was* that?" she asked Ella in alarm.

Ella shook her head. "An orca," she replied. "Also known as a killer whale." A confused look was in her eyes. "Not that orcas usually bother us mermaids. They hunt everything else in the sea, but leave us alone." She thought for a moment, then took Molly's hand. "Come on," she said. "We need to make sure the whale is all right. It's acting very oddly."

Molly gasped. She hadn't been expecting that! She wanted to get as far away from the orca as possible, not swim towards it. "Ella..." she started, but her friend was already surging through the water, pulling her along.

Ella was whistling and making strange clicking sounds to the whale, but the beast kept bucking its black head and ignoring her. "I'm just trying to calm it down," she hissed to Molly. "It's in a real state about something. I wonder if it's lost the rest of its pod – you know, its family? They don't usually travel alone like this."

But as Ella's head turned back to the whale, Molly gulped. "It's coming back," she said nervously. "Ella, get out of the way!"

Molly darted to the side, afraid of the enormous creature that was now heading straight for them once more, but Ella stayed right where she was, still making soothing clicks and whistles.

Her calming noises seemed to have no effect, though. The whale powered right on, aiming itself directly at Ella, its red eyes shining through the water in a sinister way.

Molly could hardly bear to watch as it ploughed straight into Ella and tossed her up, up, up out of the water...and out of sight!

Molly waited for her friend to splash back into the sea, but there was no sign of her. She dodged down to the seabed and hid behind a rock, trembling in fear. Where was Ella? Was she all right? And why had the whale attacked her like that? Unless... Molly remembered with a shudder how the black octopus that had tried to steal her shell necklace had had red glowing eyes too, just like the killer whale. Did that mean that the orca was part of the Dark Queen's army too?

Was that why it had attacked?

She felt very afraid for Ella. Peeping over the rock, she could see no trace of her anywhere. The orca seemed to have vanished, too. Molly swallowed, determined to be brave.

"Ella!" she shouted, swimming slowly back out into the open. "Ella, where are you?"

Silence. Molly was starting to panic. Why hadn't Ella reappeared? She surged on, pushing through the water. Fear thudded through her like a drumbeat. What if she couldn't find Ella? What if Ella was hurt? What if the orca came back for *her* next?

"Ella!" she yelled again. "Ella! Where are you?"

All she could hear was the sound of the water rushing past her ears as she swam. Then, very faintly, she thought she heard her name being called in reply.

"Molly! Help! I'm on the beach!"

Molly's eyes widened. On the beach? She pushed upwards with all her might, breaking the surface of the water with a splash. It took a moment for her eyes to adjust, but then, by the light of the moon, she could see a figure lying stranded on the sand, waving feebly in her direction.

Oh no. Ella really had been tossed right out of the water – and mermaids couldn't survive on land, surely?

Molly swam as close to the shoreline as she dared. "Ella! What should I do?" she asked.

Ella's teeth were chattering with cold. "I d-d-don't know," she said miserably. "I'm too far away to get back into the water on my own; my tail's no use on land. But if I'm not back in the sea soon, I'll d-d-die." She was panting and holding her throat, as if it were painful to speak. "I can't breathe out of the water for very long."

Molly bit her lip. "Will I turn back into a girl if I come ashore?" she asked. "Then I might be able to pull you back in."

"No, you can't do that," Ella said. "You mustn't come onto the beach, it's too dangerous. I don't know what would happen – we might both end up stuck here!"

"But I can't just leave you there!" Molly cried. "There must be some way I can get you back into the sea, some way I can—"

She broke off at Ella's urgent "Ssssshhhh!" and listened. She could just make out the sound of voices approaching. For a split second, hope flared in her heart – could some other mermaids have seen them and swum to help? – but then she realized the voices were male, and human, and definitely on land. Her heart sank.

A group of men approaching? This was not good news. Mermaids were meant to stay hidden from humans. If the men saw Ella, it would be a disaster!

Chapter Four

"Perfect night for a spot of fishing," Molly
heard one of the men say. "Look at that big old
moon up there!"

Ahh – so that's why they were coming down
to the beach. Molly could hear the tramp of
their footsteps along the cliff path now, then
noticed a couple of fishing boats tied up to a
small jetty nearby. Her heart leaped as Ella gave
a weak groan from the beach. Time was slipping

away, and still the fishermen came nearer. Gasping with the cold, she began swimming towards Ella, her head above water so she could keep an eye on her friend. But just then she felt something cold and slimy brushing against her middle and had to stifle a scream, scared for a moment that it was another of the Dark Queen's creatures, out to attack *her* this time. She clutched at the slimy thing, and sighed in panicky relief when she realized it was only a long bundle of kelp, a kind of seaweed, drifting with the current.

"Think of something, Molly," Ella murmured from where she lay collapsed on the beach, her pale gleaming body shivering, her eyes closing. "Ask your conch for help. But please be quick!"

The conch – of course! It had surprised

Molly before with its powers, when she'd
fought off the octopus. But what could it do
this time?

"Conch, help me," she whispered,
closing her fingers around the cool shell
where it hung from the chain round her
neck. It suddenly became warm in her hand,
and, as the clump of seaweed washed
against her once more, an idea suddenly
swam up into her mind.

The seaweed – maybe she could use it
like a rope? If she threw a long strand of it
to Ella, might she be able to drag her friend
back into the water with it?

Molly let go of her shell and grabbed a
long rubbery clump of the kelp. Holding
tight to one end, she hurled the other
towards Ella...but it missed by a long way,
and merely smacked down on the water.

"Use your conch," Ella said weakly, not moving at all now.

Molly bit her lip, feeling frightened. She had to get this right! Ella looked horribly pale and ill, lying there so still. This time, she held onto her shell with one hand and dragged back the seaweed rope with the other. "Conch, help me throw this to Ella," she begged, as she took careful aim.

The shell glowed brightly above the dark water for a second, and so did the rope of kelp. Molly hurled one end of it into the night sky and watched breathlessly as it sailed through the air, remembering to keep a tight hold of the other end.

Yes! The kelp rope landed just by Ella, who opened her eyes as it pattered onto the sand.

"Hold tight, Ella!" Molly called out in a low voice, hoping she was strong enough to drag her friend in before the fishermen reached the beach. And then she pulled with all her might, heaving her end of the kelp until her muscles ached with exhaustion.

At first, it seemed as if nothing would happen, but then Molly found an extra burst of energy and pulled on the kelp even harder, paddling backwards with her tail.

She was just starting to worry that the kelp rope would break when she felt a movement – and saw Ella shift slightly on the sand.

The fishermen were tramping down onto the beach now, the lights of their torches swaying like golden eyes in the darkness. Molly had to get Ella into the water before they saw her – she just had to!

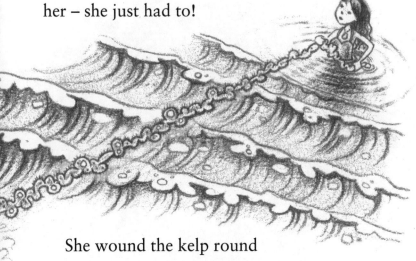

She wound the kelp round her wrists and renewed her pulling efforts. Centimetre by centimetre, Ella's body was hauled over the sand.

She was getting nearer and nearer to the sea, until...

Splash! With one last huge heave, Ella was in the water, tail and all.

"What was that?" one of the fishermen asked, peering into the sea. "Sounded like a big 'un."

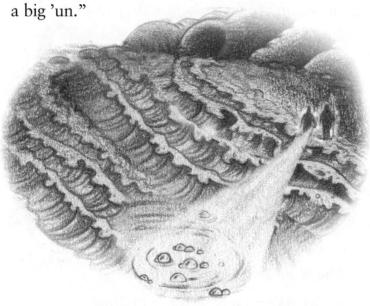

Molly ducked below the surface before they could shine their torches in her direction and swam as fast as she could to Ella. There she was, limp in the water, her blonde hair swirling all around her face like a golden feathery sea-plant. Molly felt a lurch inside at the sight of her floating so still. Was she all right? Was she still alive?

"Ella!" she called, swimming the last few strokes. "Are you okay? Can you hear me?"

She grabbed hold of her hand and towed her further into the water, away from the shore. Ella still hadn't spoken, but as Molly stopped swimming, and lifted her friend's face to look at her, Ella's eyes opened.

She blinked – once, twice – then flung her arms around Molly. "Oh, Molly!" she cried. "Thank you! You saved my life!"

Molly had tears in her eyes – tears of relief, and exhaustion. But there was still work to be done before they could rest. "I guess if you're okay, we should swim to the cave and see if your shell *is* in there," she said, glancing nervously around. "We don't want to meet that whale again. I'm sure he's one of the Dark Queen's army. Did you see his red eyes?"

Ella nodded. "Carlotta must have heard about the sparkles in the cave here, too," she said. "I bet she sent the orca along to guard it, and to stop us getting inside until she could come here and see for herself."

At those words, Molly felt very afraid. "Then we need to hurry," she said staunchly, even though her heart was pounding with fear. "We need to see if it really is your shell that's sparkling in the cave. Quick – before Carlotta comes!"

Ella nodded. "You're right," she said. "Let's go."

The two mermaids swam together to where the rocky cliff face met the sea. By now, the tide had come in and the cave would be completely submerged. They went past a buoy, anchored to the seabed, with its orange float bobbing on the surface, and the row of fishing boats moored to the jetty. They had to swim right underneath the fishing boats, dodging the nets that dangled below them.

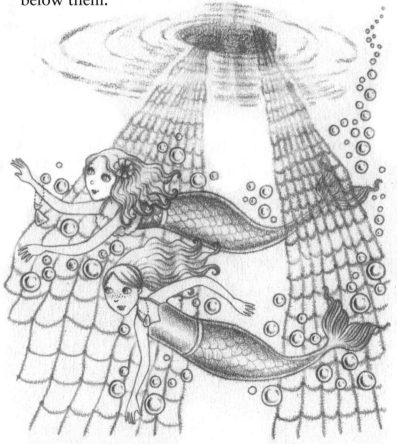

Molly flinched as she heard the heavy tread of the fishermen's boots as they got on board, and the creak of the boat timbers. Thank goodness she'd managed to pull Ella to safety before the men had seen her! They might have tried to catch her in one of those nets.

Her thoughts were interrupted by a shout of excitement from Ella as they reached the entrance to the cave. "Look! That must be what the seals were talking about."

Molly gazed ahead to where Ella was pointing, and saw a flash of bright golden sparkles on one of the rocky sides of the cave. She and Ella swam in to investigate. It was like swimming into a secret room, Molly thought to herself, peering around the dark walls. Seaweed grew in the cracks between the rocks, and limpets and barnacles clung to the sides.

And there, on one side, something very bright
was sending out a golden light, streaking the
water with hundreds of tiny golden reflections.

"I'm sure it's my shell!" Ella cried, surging through the water eagerly. Molly followed and saw that the sparkly object was wedged into a rocky crevice. A large stone was lodged above it, almost hiding it from view, and Ella's fingers scrabbled to dislodge the stone. "I just can't get it to move!" she cried hopelessly, after a few moments' frantic tugging.

Molly drew closer to see if she could help. Then she saw that her own piece of conch was sparkling and she clasped it quickly, wondering if something magical was happening. As soon as her fingers touched the smooth surface of her shell, the stone Ella had been pulling at came away easily. And there underneath was...

"My shell!" Ella cried, lifting it out happily from where it had been stuck in a hollow. She held the creamy-pink conch piece in her cupped hands, smiling in delight.

Molly stared as Ella's shell suddenly glowed
an even brighter gold, and sent dazzling sparkles
shooting out all around the water, like electrical
currents pulsing in every direction. "What's
happening?" she asked. "Is everything okay?"

Ella laughed. "Everything's perfect!" she
replied. "Now that my shell is back with me,

where it belongs, it's helping to control the tides. The floods will soon subside, and all will be well along the coastlines!"

Molly beamed. "That's fantastic," she said. "Does it really work just by you holding it?"

Ella nodded, her face wreathed in smiles. "These conch pieces are very powerful," she said, tucking it into a little pink shell-shaped bag that she wore on her wrist. "And we Shell-Keepers respect the magic powers within them and use them for the good of the ocean. Not like Carlotta! She just wants to use their magic selfishly, so that she has enough power to rule the seas." An angry look crossed her face at the thought. "Still, I've got my shell back now," she went on. "And we should take it straight back to the Undersea Kingdom, where it'll be safe again."

Molly smiled at the thought. She felt really happy and proud that she had helped Ella get her piece of the conch back. She couldn't wait to tell the Merqueen all about it.

She and Ella began swimming out of the cave. "How did your shell get stolen in the first place?" Molly asked.

"Well, that's the odd thing," Ella said. "You see—"

But she never finished her sentence. Before she could say another word, there came a great rushing of water towards them, and Ella and Molly both saw a huge dark shape powering their way.

"Oh no," Molly gulped. "It's the whale – it's come back for us!"

Chapter Five

Molly and Ella both darted back into the cave again. Fortunately, the opening was too narrow for the whale to get inside, but it cruised to and fro past the mouth of the cave instead, its red eyes glowing. They were trapped.

Ella groaned. "What are we going to do?" she asked, looking downcast. "When the tide goes out, there won't be any sea left in here."

Molly realized something else. "And as soon

as the sun rises, I'll be a human again, back in bed. And then you'll be on your own, and..."

Ella nodded, as Molly's voice trailed away. "We've got to get out," she said firmly. "Let's think. Between us, we must be able to work out a plan. Any bright ideas?"

Molly thought for a moment. "Maybe we can distract the whale somehow and send it off in the wrong direction, then make a quick escape," she suggested. "Or perhaps there's a way we could keep it from chasing after us..." She shrugged. "Is there some kind of magic we could do, to prevent it from following us?"

Ella looked uncertain. "It goes against our mermaid rules to harm a sea creature in any way," she replied, "but if we can think of something that won't hurt the whale..."

Molly suddenly remembered the way she'd used the kelp to make a rope for Ella earlier.

"What if we can somehow lasso the whale and tie it to the buoy we passed, out in the deeper water? A rope made of kelp won't hurt the whale, will it?"

"No, it won't," Ella said thoughtfully. "That might just work. Good idea!"

They peered out of the cave again to see the killer whale circling nearby. As it faced away from them for a second, Molly reached out of the cave entrance to swiftly pull up armfuls of kelp, and then she and Ella retreated to the back of the cave with it. The two mermaids worked quickly, weaving and binding the kelp to make a long, strong rope. Ella tied a loop in one end and knotted it tight to make a lasso.

She glanced out again. "I don't dare swim out to tie this loose end of our rope to the buoy," she said warily, "but we can pile rocks on it here in the cave so that it holds fast. Like this."

She wedged the rope's end into a crevice and began heaping heavy rocks on top of it. Molly helped, and soon the rope was weighted down and didn't move, however hard they tried pulling on it.

"There," Ella said. "Now to see if our plan works!"

She and Molly dodged behind some rocks at the mouth of the cave as the whale swam in their direction. It was high in the water, its blowhole out in the open air so that it could breathe.

The second its head had gone past them, Ella pulled Molly above the surface with her. Then, as the creature's tail went swishing by, Ella shouted, "Now!" and they threw the kelp lasso towards the whale's tail fin.

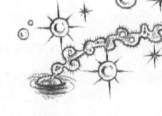

Molly clutched her conch piece instinctively, her heart racing. "Conch, guide my aim!" she called out as she let go of the lasso.

She hardly dared breathe as she and Ella watched it fly through the air and land perfectly, glowing brightly as it tightened around the black, rudder-like tail fin. Yes – they had done it!

The whale tugged impatiently at the lasso and Molly crossed her fingers, hoping that the kelp rope would hold fast for a little while. The orca snorted and bucked in the water, but couldn't move very far.

"Let's get away while we can," Ella whispered. "Quick, Molly!"

Molly didn't need telling twice. She struck out away from the orca, pushing her tail hard from side to side in order to swim faster than she'd ever done before. She didn't dare look behind, but could hear the mighty creature making furious-sounding clicks and whistles. "It doesn't sound very happy," she said nervously, hoping it wouldn't break through the rope in its rage.

"It's not," Ella replied grimly. "But it'll be fine. It'll soon work out how to bite through the kelp lasso with those monstrous teeth.

But by then, we should be safely back in the Undersea Kingdom." Her hand stole round to clutch the pink pouch containing her shell. "The main thing is, I've got my conch piece again." She turned to Molly with a smile. "And you and your conch piece helped me get it. I'm so glad you were with me, Molly. I might still have been on that beach without you."

"I'm glad I was there too," Molly replied. She could feel the magical shell bobbing against her skin as she swam, and smiled to herself. Being a mermaid was truly amazing!

It wasn't long before Molly saw the golden gates that marked the entrance to the Undersea Kingdom, where all the mermaids lived. Thank goodness! Ella quickly unlocked the gates with her tiny golden key and she and Molly swam through. They were safe! Molly felt dizzy with relief.

"Come on," Ella said, taking her by the hand. "We need to tell Queen Luna what's happened. And we must get a warning out to Coral, Delphi, Shivana and Pearl to be on their guard for the Dark Queen's army."

Molly agreed, and they swam to the mermaid palace – a grand, three-storey building carved out of dazzling white rock, with intricate towers and turrets, and fairy-tale balconies. As they swam closer, Molly started to get the feeling she was being watched, but could see no sign of anybody when she stared up at the palace windows. She gave herself a little shake. She was probably imagining things, after the scary time she'd just had with Ella.

The Merqueen herself opened the tall mother-of-pearl doors and swam out to greet them. "Welcome back!" she cried. "What news do you bring?"

Ella smiled and pulled her conch piece from the pink bag to show the Merqueen, who clapped a hand to her mouth in joy. "How wonderful!" she exclaimed. "This *is* good news. Oh, well done!"

Ella looked troubled. "I'm afraid it's not all good news, Your Majesty," she replied, and glanced around before repeating the whale story in a low voice.

Queen Luna looked very uneasy at what Ella had to say. "It does sound as if the Dark Queen has enchanted the poor beast," she said. "My guess is that Carlotta is using her dark magic to enslave creatures against their will, to form an army. For an orca to become separated from its pod, and to attack like that... It's very unusual. But aside from that..." She bestowed a brilliant smile on both Molly and Ella. "You have done well, my dears. Very well."

Molly glowed with pride and ducked her head respectfully. "Thank you," she said, a little shyly. She was still rather in awe of the powerful Merqueen.

Queen Luna glanced upwards, and pointed to a shaft of white light that had appeared, shining brightly through the water. "Dawn is now upon us," she said, taking Molly's hands. "It's time for you to return home."

"Oh no! Already?" Molly asked, feeling disappointed. "But what about the other pieces of the conch? I need to help find them too!"

The Merqueen smiled and squeezed Molly's hands gently between her own. "You are brave, secret mermaid," she said. "And we are grateful to you for all that you have done. Look after your piece of the conch and our secret, and you will return to us soon."

"But when?" Molly cried. "How will I know when I can come back? I've got so many questions I—"

"Until next time,"
the Merqueen
promised. "Farewell!"

"Goodbye!"
Molly said. "Oh,
goodbye!" She just
had time to hug
Ella and bob a
little curtsy to the
Merqueen before
she had the sensation
of being pulled very
fast to the surface of
the ocean, with the mermaid
world rushing and blurring in
front of her eyes.

Chapter Six

"Goodbye! Goodbye!" Molly murmured
thickly, rolling over. She opened her eyes,
expecting to see Ella's smiling face and the
Merqueen's majestic beauty before her...but
instead found that she was staring into her own
pillow. She was back home, in her own bed.

Molly lay still for a few moments, while the
racing of her heart subsided. What an
adventure! It felt like a roller-coaster ride –

a mixture of scariness and excitement...not to mention the sheer relief she'd felt at the end.

She sat up, rubbing her eyes. There was her conch shell, lying on her pillow where she'd left it, its chain coiled neatly around it. And... She blinked. Oh! There on her wrist was what looked like a bracelet, made of woven kelp.

She wriggled her hand out of it and looked at it closely, fingering it and sniffing it. It smelled of the sea. Definitely kelp.

She smiled to herself, then put it next to her conch necklace. Being a secret mermaid was just so wonderful!

She pulled on her dressing gown and ran down the narrow little staircase to the kitchen, where she could smell hot toast and bacon. "You look very cheerful this morning," her mum commented as Molly skipped into the room and sat down at the table.

Her gran peered curiously at her. "Nice dreams?" she asked, with interest.

Molly nodded. "Very exciting," she replied, knowing not to say anything more about it.

The radio was burbling as Molly's mum passed her a plate of bacon and egg. "...And our forecaster, David Harris, says the threat of coastal flooding is now over, with normal tides once again..." the radio presenter said chattily. "So no need to worry about getting your feet wet any more! Now, on to this morning's travel news..."

Molly couldn't help a rush of happiness and pride at the radio presenter's words. No more coastal flooding, he'd said – and she was sure that was because she'd helped Ella get her piece of conch shell back! She glanced out of the kitchen window, where she could just see the sea, its waves curling onto the sand halfway up the beach. It was a beautiful day out there – blue sky, and no clouds, with the sun making the waves sparkle with golden light.

She turned back to her breakfast and noticed that Gran was smiling at her across the table. "Glad to hear the floods have receded," Gran said conversationally, and gave Molly a deliberate wink.

"Me too," said Molly and grinned back at her. Oh, it was *so* exciting being a secret mermaid! She couldn't wait for her next mermaid adventure!

The End

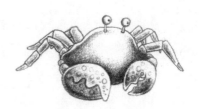

*Read on for a sneak
preview of Molly's next
magical underwater
adventure...*

Underwater Magic

Molly had been a mermaid twice before now,
but she still wasn't used to the peculiar melting
sensation as her body transformed. Her legs in
particular felt as if they were dissolving into
nothing – it was rather alarming! But then,
suddenly, she could feel the coolness of seawater
against her skin and she opened her eyes eagerly.
Yes! She was a mermaid again. Her legs had
vanished, and now she had her very own
shimmering silver tail flicking behind her!

"Hello, Molly," came a voice from nearby. "I thought that was you!"

Molly turned to see Delphi, one of the other Shell-Keeper mermaids. Delphi had bobbed auburn hair, green eyes and a sprinkling of freckles over her nose. She wore a jade-green top, and had a pale green flower tucked in her hair.

"Hello!" Molly cried joyfully and swam over towards her. Something felt different though. Why was it so hard to swim all of a sudden? Usually, as a mermaid, Molly could speed through the water very fast.

Delphi noticed Molly struggle and came to meet her halfway. "The current is really strong today, isn't it?" she said. She hugged Molly in welcome. "There have been some terrible storms lately, too. Usually, my piece of the conch helps me protect sailors at sea – I can use its powers to guide their ships safely back to harbour. But without it, I haven't been able to do anything, and there have almost been some dreadful shipwrecks."

"Well, I can help you look for your shell," Molly said at once. "I— "

Before she could finish her sentence, though, a pod of dolphins had appeared, smiling as they dived down through the water towards the two mermaids.

"Ahh," Delphi murmured to Molly. "Here come my little helpers. Or rather, they *think* they're helping."

The first dolphin to reach them made some excited whistling, snickering noises to Delphi, its eyes bright and alert. Molly couldn't take her eyes off the beautiful creature. She could hardly believe she was so close to it!

"You think you've found the shell?" Delphi replied. "Okay, we'll follow you. Come on,

Molly, let's see what they've got this time."

She flicked her tail fin and surged away through the water. Molly gave her own tail a sharp wiggle and swam after her. She was surprised that Delphi didn't seem more enthusiastic at the dolphin's message. "What's up?" she hissed to her as they followed the sleek, silvery dolphins.

Delphi gave a tired smile in reply. "I do love the dolphins – they're so cheerful and bouncy and keen to help," she said in a low voice, "but they're a bit *too* keen to help, if you know what I mean. They've been in and out of the shipwrecks looking for my conch piece, and they keep thinking they've seen it, and coming to get me, when really it's just another piece of human treasure that they've discovered." She rolled her eyes comically. "What with them, and Princess Silva hanging around all the time asking if I've found the shell yet, I've hardly had a minute to myself."

Molly bit her lip, hoping she would be more help than the dolphins and Princess Silva. Maybe Delphi didn't even *want* her hanging around – maybe she was secretly wishing Molly hadn't turned up at all!

Delphi caught the doubtful expression on Molly's face and put a hand on her arm. "Oh – I didn't mean I wanted to be on my own *now*!" she said quickly. "I heard how brilliant you were at helping Ella when she'd been thrown onto the sand by that scary killer whale. I'm really pleased you're here to help me, too – truly, Molly!"

Molly smiled in relief. "Oh good," she said. "I'm pleased to be here."

They swam on, and Molly remembered Delphi's earlier comment about Princess Silva, daughter of the Merqueen. Queen Luna was lovely, but there was something a bit odd about the princess, Molly thought privately. She always seemed to be hanging around in the background, listening and watching without saying very much. Maybe she was just a bit shy, though.

The dolphins had stopped before a huge rock on the seabed and were pointing their shiny noses at it, all making whistling noises at once.

"Okay, let's have a look," Delphi said in a good-humoured way. Molly could tell she didn't really believe her shell would be there.

But then Delphi's mouth fell open in surprise and her eyes lit up. "Oh! My conch! You really *did* find it!" she cried, and she threw her arms around the nearest dolphin, covering his head with happy kisses.

Molly swam over to the rock excitedly for a closer look. Sure enough, wedged into a crevice was Delphi's piece of the conch! The shell's creamy surface seemed to glow against the dark, barnacle-covered rock, and was half-hidden by a spiky round object that rested on top of it. Was the spiky thing some kind of plant? Molly wondered.

Delphi patted the other dolphins lovingly, then joined Molly in front of the rock. "At last!" she cried happily, reaching out a hand to move the spiky thing. "Oh, I've been so worried! And now—"

"Oi!" the spiky thing snapped in a bad-tempered way, making Molly jump back in alarm. "Get your hand away from me, or I'll jab you with my spines!"

Molly stared at the spiky thing and then questioningly at Delphi. "What *is* that?" she whispered.

"It's a sea urchin," Delphi replied in a low voice. "A grumpy sea urchin at that!" She turned back to the creature. "But you're on my shell," she said to it politely. "Please would you move, so that I can get it?"

"No," the sea urchin told her. "It's mine now, I found it. Lovely and smooth it is, too, after that craggy old rock. Shouldn't have been so careless with it, should you?"

"Oh please," Molly put in. "It was stolen from her – she wasn't being careless!"

The sea urchin's red spines rippled in the current. They did look horribly sharp, Molly thought to herself. "I said no, and I mean no!" the sea urchin replied crossly.

To find out what happens next, read

To find out more
about Molly and all her
mermaid friends, and have
some magical ocean fun,
check out

www.thesecretmermaid.co.uk

Collect all of Molly's magical mermaid adventures

Enchanted Shell ◎ 9780746096154

Molly is transported to the Undersea Kingdom for the first time, where she discovers she is the secret mermaid!

Seaside Adventure ◎ 9780746096161

To help Ella recover her piece of the magical conch, Molly must find a way to trap an angry killer whale.

Underwater Magic ◎ 9780746096178

Can Molly find some pirate treasure to win back Delphi's shell from a grumpy sea urchin?

Reef Rescue ◎ 9780746096192

Molly must help Coral find her shell to restore the ocean reefs, but a swarm of jellyfish stands in their way…

Deep Trouble ◎ 9780746096185

Pearl's conch piece is trapped in an undersea volcano and guarded by sea snakes. How can she and Molly release it?

Return of the Dark Queen ◎ 9780746096208

Molly must save Shivana from an Arctic prison before the Shell-Keeper mermaids can finally face the Dark Queen and complete the magical conch.

Seahorse SOS ⊙ 9781409506324

There's more trouble in the Undersea Kingdom and Molly joins in the search for the missing seahorses.

Dolphin Danger ⊙ 9781409506331

Molly and Aisha can hear faint calls for help but the dolphins are nowhere to be seen. Where can they be?

Penguin Peril ⊙ 9781409506348

Could the Dark Queen be behind the mysterious disappearance of the penguins from the icy seas?

Turtle Trouble ⊙ 9781409506355

There are some scary monsters lurking in the coral reef and they're guarding the turtles Molly has come to set free!

Whale Rescue ⊙ 9781409506393

Molly must not only save the trapped whales but also her mermaid friend, Leila.

The Dark Queen's Revenge ⊙ 9781409506409

The Dark Queen is back and she wants to rule the Undersea Kingdom with her bad magic. Can Molly put an end to her vile plans?

Oliver Moon
Junior Wizard

Collect all of Oliver Moon's magical adventures!

Oliver Moon and the Potion Commotion
Can Oliver create a potion to win the Young Wizard of the Year award? ISBN 9780746073063

Oliver Moon and the Dragon Disaster
Oliver's sure his new pet dragon will liven up the Festival of Magic... ISBN 9780746073070

Oliver Moon and the Nipperbat Nightmare
Things go horribly wrong when Oliver gets to look after the school pet. ISBN 9780746077917

Oliver Moon's Summer Howliday
Oliver suspects there is something odd about his hairy new friend, Wilf. ISBN 9780746077924

Oliver Moon's Christmas Cracker
Can a special present save Oliver's Christmas at horrible Aunt Wart's? ISBN 9780746077931

Oliver Moon and the Spell-off
Oliver must win a spell-off against clever Casper to avoid a scary forfeit. ISBN 9780746077948

Oliver Moon's Fangtastic Sleepover

Will Oliver survive a school sleepover in the haunted house museum?

ISBN 9780746084793

Oliver Moon and the Broomstick Battle

Can Oliver beat Bully to win the Junior Wizards' Obstacle Race?

ISBN 9780746084809

Happy Birthday, Oliver Moon

Will Oliver's birthday party be ruined when his invitations go astray?

ISBN 9780746086872

Oliver Moon and the Spider Spell

Oliver's Grow-bigger spell lands the Witch Baby's pet in huge trouble.

ISBN 9780746090749

Oliver Moon and the Troll Trouble

Can Oliver save the show as the scary, stinky troll in the school play?

ISBN 9780746086865

Oliver Moon and the Monster Mystery

Strange things start to happen when Oliver wins a monster raffle prize...

ISBN 9780746090756

Sue Mongredien has published over 60 books, including the magical *Oliver Moon, Junior Wizard* series. Like Molly Holmes, Sue loves exploring, and gave up a job as an editor of children's books to travel the world, before becoming a full-time writer. Sue also loves the sea, and had a house near Brighton beach before moving to Bath, where she now lives with her husband and three children.

For more enchanting adventures
log on to
www.fiction.usborne.com